►► RACE TO THE TOP ◄◄

BY MICHAEL ANTHONY STEELE

ILLUSTRATED BY MIKE LAUGHEAD

raintree

a Capstone company — publishers for children

Raintree is an imprint of Capstone Global Library Limited, a company incorporated in England and Wales having its registered office at 264 Banbury Road, Oxford, OX2 7DY – Registered company number: 6695582

Designed by Heidi Thompson
Original illustrations © Capstone Global Library Limited 2025
Originated by Capstone Global Library Ltd

978 1 3982 5750 4

British Library Cataloguing in Publication Data
A full catalogue record for this book is available from the British Library.

Printed and bound in India.

CONTENTS

CHAPTER 1
MONSTER TRUCK MASH 8

CHAPTER 2
RACER RESCUE 15

CHAPTER 3
BIG ANNOUNCEMENT 21

CHAPTER 4
FALLING STAR 25

CHAPTER 5
IN NEED OF REPAIRS 32

CHAPTER 6
STAGE TIME 36

CHAPTER 7
BIG DECISION 40

CHAPTER 8
TIMBER! 47

CHAPTER 9
THE BIG NEWS 54

CHAPTER 10
LAST RACE 58

OPEN WORLD

In this online video game, players are free. Be whatever avatar you want. Team up with whoever you want. Choose any type of mission you want! Fantasy adventure, battle racing, sci-fi, action and more. So log on . . .

Open World awaits!

THE SQUAD

Kai

Screen name: K-EYE
Avatar: Techno-Ninja
Strengths: Supply,
Stealth

Kai doesn't like being the centre of
attention. He chose a role in OW where
he can help others – in the background.
His ninja avatar has many pockets to hold
the squad's gear. Kai takes the job very
seriously. He is quick to rush into a fight
and pass out anything the group needs.

Hanna

Screen name:
hanna_banana
Avatar: Elvin Archer
Strengths: Speed,
Long-Range Attacks

Hanna is often busy with her school's drama
department. She first joined OW to spend
more time with her best friend, Zoe. In OW,
she's great with a bow and arrow. Hanna
is thrilled to take on a big role during the
squad's attacks.

Mason

Screen name: MACE1
Avatar: Robo-Warrior
Strengths: Leadership,
Close-Range
Attacks

Mason knows the value of teamwork.
So he and his best friend, Kai, teamed up
in OW with cross-country friends Hanna
and Zoe. Mason has a strong avatar. But his
true strength? Acting as squad leader and
bringing together the players' many skills.

Zoe

Screen name: ZKatt
Avatar: Feline Wizard
Strengths: Spells,
Defence

Zoe is a tech wizard and OW expert.
She has been playing for the longest time
out of everyone in the squad. Her avatar's
magic and defence skills help to keep the
group safe. Zoe isn't quite a pro gamer.
But she's close! Hundreds of followers
watch her live streams.

CHAPTER 1

MONSTER TRUCK MASH

Hanna hit the accelerator. Her monster truck sped off the ramp. **VROOOM!** Her engine roared in mid-air.

CRASH!

She landed on an enemy racer. She bounced off the smashed car. Then back onto the road.

Hanna laughed as she watched the action on her computer screen. She hadn't been sure about this mission at first. Now? She was having the time of her life!

That was the great thing about Open World. The online video game had lots of missions to choose from. You could take down bad guys in the Wild West. Defeat dragons in a fantasy level. Or even race through a wrecked city.

Like Hanna and her squad were doing right now.

It was one of several exciting races. All the vehicles had battle weapons and special mods. The track had almost no rules.

Hanna and her three friends were up against a dozen NPC drivers. Every race led them closer to the level's main goal. The finish line at the top of a snowy mountain.

Hanna drove up a crumbling on-ramp. She dropped through a hole and landed on the side of a fallen skyscraper. The large building leaned against a smaller one. Hanna raced towards the top. Broken glass sprayed out from under her tyres.

"This racetrack is crazy," Hanna mumbled. Then a chat box popped up on her screen.

ZKatt: H? where ru?

hanna_banana: on yur 6!

Hanna zoomed past Zoe. Her best friend and teammate drove a dune buggy. The small car bounced slightly as it zipped along. Both girls sped off the skyscraper. Hanna's truck slammed onto a nearby overpass.

But wings popped out of Zoe's buggy. She glided through the air.

BOOM! BOOM-BOOM!

Zoe dropped bombs onto enemy cars below. Critical hit! The NPC drivers were out of the race.

A second later, the buggy landed on the overpass. The wings folded away.

Zoe was the squad's most skilled member. Almost a pro gamer! She sometimes even live streamed their missions to her many followers. Of course *she* wouldn't have an ordinary vehicle.

> **hanna_banana:** i SO shoulda picked the buggy
>
> **ZKatt:** and give up your spears?
>
> **hanna_banana:** lol!!! tru dat!

Hanna fired a giant spear from her monster truck. **FWOP!** The spear hit its target. It pinned an enemy car to a building.

Hanna caught up to an armoured van. That was Kai. Another member of their squad. As always, Kai was in charge of supplies.

> **hanna_banana:** more spears plz K!
>
> **ZKatt:** got bombs too?
>
> **K-EYE:** Yep and yep. On it!

The van door slid open. A bundle of spears flew out. It hit Hanna's truck and disappeared. Then came cartoony bombs. They disappeared into the buggy.

ZKatt: thx!

MACE1: cud use some hlp up here

hanna_banana: coming!!!

Hanna sped through the ruined buildings. She quickly found Mason. He was the fourth squad member. Three enemy racers surrounded his muscle car. They had him boxed in.

FWOOSH! Flames blasted from the sides of Mason's car. But the other racers didn't go down.

FWOP! Hanna fired a spear. It knocked out the left enemy car.

Mason rammed the right car. It smashed into a building.

That left only one car in front.

Hanna grinned. She knew just how to take care of it. She hit the accelerator. Shot up a fallen billboard. Flew off the sign and over Mason's car. Then –

CRASH! She landed on the last enemy racer.

MACE1: u almost hit ME

hanna_banana: ur welcome!!!

The squad raced out of the city. Hanna led the way. They zipped up another on-ramp. The end of the first race was in sight. Just one more turn!

But the last turn was sharp. Kai's heavy van didn't make it. He slammed on the brakes. It wasn't enough. His vehicle slid and broke through a guardrail. The van teetered on the edge of the road.

K-EYE: Help!!!

CHAPTER 2

RACER RESCUE

SCREEECH!

Hanna hit the brakes. She spun around and raced back towards Kai.

ZKatt: plan???

hanna_banana: keep going, i got this!

Mason and Zoe moved to the side as Hanna drove the wrong way. The enemy racers weren't as polite. They tried to smash into her. Hanna dodged their attacks.

Another NPC's car closed in. But it was heading sraight for Kai. It was going to ram him off the road!

Hanna loaded a special spear. **FWOOP!**
It punched into Kai's van.

> **K-EYE:** You shot me!
>
> **hanna_banana:** yup! hang on

This spear had a long cable tied to it. Hanna began reversing. The cable went tight. She pulled Kai away from the edge. She was just in time.

The enemy car rushed forwards. It sailed through the gap in the guardrail. It smashed onto the ground below. **KA-BOOM!**

Hanna dropped the cable. She and Kai zoomed down the road. Ahead, Mason and Zoe had already crossed the finish line. Hanna and Kai followed. Race one done!

Hanna's screen filled with the racers' scores. Her squad had come in fourth place. That earned them a nice amount of Open World credits.

They could use the credits between races. They could buy upgrades. Repairs. Weapons. And the higher the squad placed? The more credits they earned.

The scene on Hanna's screen changed. It now showed a repair depot. NPC drivers each stood by their vehicles. So did the squad's avatars.

There was Mason's robot-head warrior and his muscle car. Zoe's wizard cat and her buggy. Kai's techno-ninja and his armoured van. Hanna's tall Elvin archer and her huge monster truck.

K-EYE: Thanks for the save H! Even if you did shoot me.

hanna_banana: np, no 1 left behind!

The entire squad didn't have to cross the finish line. But if one of them didn't, he or she would have to run that race over again. Alone. Without any credits.

Besides, the players made a perfect team. It was worth making sure everyone finished. They would all do better if they faced the course together.

MACE1: no 1 left bhind? u almost squashed me H!

hanna_banana: but i didnt, i saved u!!!

MACE1: well ur buyin repairs if u squish me nxt time

hanna_banana: u bet! ;)

ZKatt: srsly tho nice driving H. and u had doubts about a racing level

hanna_banana: i guess my IRL skillz frm driving ranch ATVs came in handy. who knew?

K-EYE: Forgot you live on a ranch. Nice.

hanna_banana: used 2

Hanna glanced around her new room. Most of her things were still in boxes. It hardly felt like home.

hanna_banana: i just moved n with grandparents while dad gets ready 2 sell

K-EYE: Why is he selling?

hanna_banana: new job in the city, so no time 2 take care of the ranch :(

MACE1: that suks. my parents wrk all the time and thats tuff enuf

hanna_banana: im ok. dad calls a lot and my gramps r gr8! the new school is super weird tho, its BIG

ZKatt: i miss my bestie!! but u make friends so easy, i bet u already replaced me lol

hanna_banana: NEVER!!! rly tho school is crazy. im a theatre nerd but new drama group is SO HUGE that im still learning ppls names :(

ZKatt: everyone will know YOUR name when ur the star of the next show!

hanna_banana: lol idk, more competition here

MACE1: ur the best actor i know

hanna_banana: i bet im the only actor you know

MACE1: doesnt mean ur not the best!

hanna_banana: lol thx!!!

K-EYE: Ready to resupply for next race?

MACE1: ok with supply + repairs, but save next race for tomorrw? almost dinnertime

hanna_banana: gr8!!! cant w8!!!

Hanna sighed as she logged off. Really, she wanted to play longer. She was a little nervous about tomorrow. Her new drama department was going to announce what the play for the new term was going to be.

Usually, Hanna would be thrilled. But everything felt just a bit off at her new school. *She* felt off. Like she didn't quite fit in.

So right now? Hanna could use all the distraction she could get.

CHAPTER 3

BIG ANNOUNCEMENT

"There've been many fine ideas for our next play," Mrs Bruening said. The drama teacher pushed up her glasses. "I've weighed the pros and cons of each one."

Hanna leaned forwards in her seat. The other drama students did the same. The large group filled four rows in the auditorium. Everyone was there after school to hear the big announcement.

"I've decided to go with a classic," Mrs Bruening continued. "Our next play will be . . . *Oklahoma!*"

The reaction was mixed. Lots of happy chatter. A few groans. Hanna felt torn herself.

The girl next to her turned. "Hey, didn't you say you did *Oklahoma!* at your old school?" Erica asked.

Erica was one name Hanna *did* know. Everyone knew Erica. She was outgoing. And really nice.

Hanna nodded. "I did," she said. "I played Laurey."

Erica's eyes widened. "One of the leads. Wow."

That was why Hanna was torn. She had been hoping to do a new play. So part of her was disappointed. But she was also excited. She already knew *Oklahoma!* really well. She could nail the lead again. Be the star. As usual.

"I'm going to throw a curveball at you, though!" Mrs Bruening called out. The students went quiet. "We've already been doing practice auditions in class. So, these real auditions will start tomorrow."

That caused a stir. "You don't have to use a piece from *Oklahoma!*," the teacher added. "Choose any play you want. Any scene. In the real world, actors don't always get time to prepare for auditions. So, we're trying that here."

Mrs Bruening spent the rest of the time helping students. She answered questions and gave advice.

Hanna didn't need to talk to the teacher. Instead, she dug out her phone. She logged into the OW mobile app. She sent a chat request to Zoe.

hanna_banana: its official, we r doing oklahoma

ZKatt: great! u were so good in it!

hanna_banana: thx, tho i was kinda hoping 4 something new

ZKatt: so ur not auditioning?

hanna_banana: OF COURSE I M!!!

ZKatt: yull get the lead 4 sure!

hanna_banana: idk Erica was the lead in their last play. ppl say shes really good

ZKatt: a differnt part could b fun? something new 2 u at least?

hanna_banana: oh im still going for the lead!

ZKatt: have 2 b the star huh? ;)

hanna_banana: u know it! a star has to shine!!!

ZKatt: speaking of being the star, i chatted the guys and they said it was ok to stream our OW mission. that ok with u?

hanna_banana: sure but whats that got to do with being a star?

ZKatt: cuz w/ yur driving skills, yull b the star of our next race!

CHAPTER 4

FALLING STAR

CRUNCH!

Later that day, Hanna drove over an enemy racer. Her monster truck smashed it flat.

> **K-EYE:** Another one bites the dust!

> **hanna_banana:** howd yur followers like that killer move Z? >:)

> **ZKatt:** they r going wild!

Hanna smiled. She couldn't see chats from the live stream. And Zoe's followers couldn't see the squad's messages.

Still, Hanna knew hundreds of people were watching her every move. Her heart raced with excitement.

It was the level's second race. This track twisted through a ruined suburb. Enemy cars kept bursting out of side streets. But they were no match for Hanna's monster truck. She simply drove over them.

The squad zoomed forwards. They worked their way through the maze of streets.

FOOM! A missile suddenly fired from a wrecked house. It slammed into Kai. His van leaned to one side. But it landed back on the road and kept moving.

K-EYE: Uh what was that?

hanna_banana: rocket launcher frm house

As soon as Hanna had typed the words, another one fired. The rocket flew straight at her truck. Hanna swerved. The rocket just missed.

More rockets fired as they raced through the streets. **FOOM! FOOM-FOOM! FOOM!**

The four friends weren't the only ones under attack. The rockets took out two NPC cars.

FWOP! Hanna took out a third with a spear.

Hanna and her squad powered ahead. They took the lead!

An enemy car pulled up alongside Hanna's monster truck. **FWOOSH!** It fired a flamethrower.

Hanna frowned. "Don't attack them, but they can still attack us," she said to herself.

She swerved at the car, trying to squash it.

It dodged. **FWOOSH!** More fire. More damage.

"Come on," Hanna said. She tried to smash the car again. No luck.

K-EYE: I see the finish line!

MACE1: LETS GOOO

Hanna hardly read the chat. She was focused on the annoying flamethrower car. It darted down a side street. She followed. She was thinking of Zoe's followers. They would want a show. She couldn't let them down. So she couldn't let this guy get away!

MACE1: H???

ZKatt: where ru going???

Hanna didn't reply. She would take out the enemy. Then catch up with the others. She lined up her spear.

FWOP! Miss! She moved closer. There was no way she would miss the next shot.

Her target took another hard turn. Hanna followed. They came into a ruined football stadium.

As soon as she drove onto the field, Hanna knew she had made a mistake. A wooden gate dropped behind her. Rockets shot down from the stands.

FOOM! FOOM-FOOM-FOOM! FOOM!

It was a trap!

Hanna drove her truck in a wide circle on the field. She barely kept ahead of the rockets. She wanted to chat for help. But it was all she could do to keep from getting blown up!

Her heart beat faster. She didn't see a way out of this.

CRASH!

Kai's van burst through the gate. He blocked two rockets as he joined Hanna on the field.

Then Zoe's buggy glided over the stands. **BOOM!** **BOOM-BOOM!** She dropped several bombs before landing on the grass.

Mason's car entered last. He skidded to a stop beside the enemy vehicle. **FWOOSH!** He gave the NPC a taste of its own medicine.

hanna_banana: thx and sry!!!

MACE1: get out of here!

The squad sped through the broken gate. They raced down the streets. But when they crossed the finish line, they were no longer in first.

They took sixth place. Second-to-last. They had earned almost no credits.

CHAPTER 5

IN NEED OF REPAIRS

At the next depot, the squad's avatars stood beside their vehicles. Hanna's monster truck showed a lot of damage.

MACE1: wut happend? we coulda got 1st!

ZKatt: instead we got 6

K-EYE: And basically zero credits for next race. It'll be tough.

hanna_banana: sry i just rly wanted to get that car

ZKatt: and it totally tricked u n2 a trap!

hanna_banana: but it made for gr8 streaming right?

MACE1: woulda been gr8r if we won

ZKatt: def

hanna_banana: thot u wanted 2 show off my skillz??

ZKatt: skillz @ getting trapped?

Hanna's lips tightened. It wasn't like that had been her plan. Why was everyone ganging up on her? Her fingers raced over the keyboard.

hanna_banana: so what wuz all that star of the show talk then???

ZKatt: so u were showing off?

hanna_banana: a little, sure! 4 the stream!

MACE1: but we r still a team tho

K-EYE: True

hanna_banana: rly dnt need ths right now

ZKatt: wdym?

K-EYE: Everything ok?

ZKatt: ru strssed bout your audition?

MACE1: ?

ZKatt: H has auditions tmrrw for new play

K-EYE: That would stress me out!

MACE1: yeah nerves alwys throw off my game

hanna_banana: if u r gonna talk about me like im not here, let me make it easy 4 u. gotta practise anywy!

ZKatt: wait!

Hanna logged off the game. The Open World logo filled her screen. She leaned back in her chair. How could her friends gang up on her like that?

DING!

Hanna looked at her phone. Zoe was texting her.

u ok?

can we talk?

sry!

Hanna didn't answer. She put her phone on silent and stood in front of her mirror.

She was angry. But she really did want to practise. She closed her eyes and breathed in deeply.

When Hanna had first started performing, she often got stage fright. But she had learned to control it. She put that nervous energy into her acting instead.

She had never tried to do the same thing with frustration or anger. Hanna opened her eyes. They filled with tears as she stared back at herself.

CHAPTER 6

STAGE TIME

The next day at school, Hanna went over her lines in her head. Then after school, she auditioned for real.

She acted out her short scene in front of the other drama students. She still had a lot of *Oklahoma!* memorized. So she did one of Laurey's scenes. In it, the character talked about all the fine things she wanted in life.

Hanna didn't miss a word. The students all clapped politely.

After that, she sang one of Laurey's songs. The students clapped again.

Hanna took a seat next to Erica. "Great job," Erica whispered.

Hanna smiled. "Thanks."

She didn't think it was that good. Yes, she hadn't missed a line. But she hadn't been totally focused.

As Hanna had said the words, part of her wondered. What did *she* really want? Did she really have to be the star?

It wasn't long before Erica took the stage. She auditioned with *Shrek The Musical*. Her scene was funny, so she got laughs. She sang her song perfectly. The students clapped. Some even threw in whistles.

Hanna clapped with everyone else. She was happy for Erica nailing the audition. But it made her more unsure of her own.

After auditions, Hanna waited for her grandfather to pick her up. She got out her phone to chat with Zoe.

hanna_banana: hey

ZKatt: ru ok?

hanna_banana: did audition

ZKatt: im sure u were great! wish i coulda seen it

hanna_banana: it went ok. everyone was good but Erica was best by far

ZKatt: u never know

hanna_banana: sry i got mad, sry 4 ghosting

ZKatt: my fault. shouldnt have pushed the star of the stream thing, especially w/ auditions so close

hanna_banana: sok. i WAS showing off tho

hanna_banana: and being new at school has just been getting to me

ZKatt: ?

hanna_banana: everything feels so dffernt. maybe i wanted the lead so 1 thing wud b normal. just wanted to prove myself and fit n

ZKatt: well no matter what u fit in great w/ your OW squad

hanna_banana: even after yesterday?

ZKatt: ESPECIALLY. evry1 gets it. we got your back!

hanna_banana: thx :)

ZKatt: so ready 2 get back in the race?

hanna_banana: YES!!! b there whn I get home

ZKatt: awk question, but care if i stream the last 2 races? my followers actually did love our rescue mission teamwork

hanna_banana: lol u bet. u wont have 2 rescue me again tho, no more showin off!!!

Hanna put her phone away. She let out a long sigh and smiled.

Who knew what would happen at her new school. Or with the play. But she did know she could always count on her squad. She was going to make sure they could always count on her too!

CHAPTER 7

BIG DECISION

That night, Hanna logged onto OW. Her knee bounced as the game loaded. She hoped her squad would be as forgiving as Zoe had said. Her avatar joined the others in the depot.

hanna_banana: hi!

MACE1: welcome back!

K-EYE: How did the audition go?

hanna_banana: ugh fine I guess

K-EYE: I bet you rocked!

ZKatt: thats what i said

MACE1: no doubt

hanna_banana: thx! and sry about the xtra drama. i was more stressed than i thot

K-EYE: It's hard being the new kid. I know!

MACE1: K barely talked to anyone when he gt here last year

K-EYE: M was the only one who talked to me!

MACE1: now K talks to at least 5 ppl!

K-EYE: LOL true!

hanna_banana: lol :)

MACE1: evry1 rdy to race?

K-EYE: Yes!

ZKatt: >:)

hanna_banana: YES!!!

The squad geared up as best they could. They had very few credits after their last race. They were able to grab a few weapons. But Hanna did not have any credits left for repairs. Her truck was still a mess.

Hanna would have to be on top of her game. She couldn't take many more hits.

The squad's vehicles lined up at the starting line. Enemy racers filled the other positions.

A desert wasteland stretched out ahead of them. It was the third race of the level. The mountaintop, their final goal, loomed even closer in the distance.

A countdown appeared on Hanna's screen.

3 . . . 2 . . . 1 . . . GO!

Dirt sprayed up as all the racers revved. Some enemies pulled ahead. Others attacked.

FWOOSH! Mason blasted one car with his flamethrower. **BAM!** Kai slammed into another. The NPC slid off the road.

Zoe's dune buggy hit a bump and flew into the air. Its wings popped out. Zoe dropped a bomb onto an enemy racer. **BOOM!**

Hanna brought up the rear. She aimed a spear. **FWOP!** It struck another enemy.

No sooner had Hanna read words than the ground dipped. Rock walls rose up on either side of her. The track led deeper into the canyon. The walls got taller. Closer.

BAM-BAM! Hanna and an enemy slammed together like bumper cars. She turned hard. **CRUNCH!** She drove right over the other racer.

Kai swerved his van. An enemy car wasn't so quick. It crashed into a giant boulder.

FOOM! FOOM-FOOM!

Rockets suddenly fired down from the top of the canyon.

"Right," Hanna muttered.

She couldn't get distracted by fighting back. And her truck couldn't take many more hits. The squad had to get out of the canyon as quickly as possible. It maybe wasn't as exciting for Zoe's stream. But it was best for the team.

The squad zipped down the narrow road.

CRUNCH! An enemy racer swerved into Mason. Another came up from behind. They pinned him against a boulder.

FOOM! FOOM! Rockets started raining down. Mason was a sitting duck!

Kai and Zoe drove past the pile-up. **FWOOSH!**
Mason blasted his flamethrower at the enemies.
They took some damage but didn't move. More rockets
slammed into Mason.

As Hanna came up to the scene, she spotted her
teammate. Mason's car was almost totally wrecked.
Then she saw a mound of earth nearby. It looked like
a ramp.

Hanna bit her lip. She didn't want to *show off* for
Zoe's followers. But she might be able to nail a tricky
move that would save Mason.

Trouble was, would she be doing it for her friend?
Or for the glory? She wasn't sure what to do.

CHAPTER 8

TIMBER!

Hanna sped towards the dirt mound. She had to try to save Mason. She flew off the mound and into the air.

VROOOM! Her engine roared. Her truck tilted as she zoomed towards the canyon wall. Her tyres hit the wall and bounced off. Her truck levelled out.

SMASH!

She landed straight on top of one of the enemy cars. Mason was free!

MACE1: thx!

hanna_banana: np!!!

Hanna and Mason raced away from more rockets. They caught up with the others.

K-EYE: Nice one H!

ZKatt: pro moves girl!

Hanna didn't reply. She focused on dodging more rockets. Soon, the road widened. It led upwards. The squad raced out of the canyon.

The road kept rising as they came to the base of the mountain. The scenery changed from rocky to green. Trees grew all around. The squad spread out on the dark forest path.

K-EYE: What's OW going to throw at us now?

BAM! There was an explosion up ahead. A tall tree started falling towards the track. It would block their path. If it didn't crush the squad first!

hanna_banana: u had 2 ask

K-EYE: My bad!

MACE1: gun it!

The squad poured on the speed. They barely slipped under the falling tree.

BAM! BA-BAM! BAM! More explosions. More trees fell towards the track.

ZKatt: TIMBERRRRR

The squad drove as fast as they could. They were now racing falling trees as well as NPC drivers.

One enemy smacked into Zoe. She lost speed. She didn't get through before the next tree fell.

But Zoe didn't need to drive on the road. She hit a bump, and her buggy bounced. The wings popped out. **SHUNK!** She glided over the huge tree trunk.

hanna_banana: pro moves yurself!

ZKatt: thx!

The group raced up the mountain and straight to the next finish line. They hadn't taken down many NPC cars. But since they hadn't stopped to fight, something better happened. They took second place!

The scene shifted to the depot. Mason's car had the most damage this time.

MACE1: thx again 4 the save back there H

hanna_banana: wasnt showing off honest :)

MACE1: lol im glad u did!

ZKatt: my followers r blowing up about ur jump

hanna_banana: mine? wut about yours??? SO COOL

ZKatt: that 2 ngl :)

K-EYE: Hey check this out!

Kai's avatar stood by a glowing item. It was a tyre covered in spikes.

MACE1: thts new

hanna_banana: think we need them for final race?

ZKatt: def. those are gonna come in handy 4 going up a snowy mountain!!

K-EYE: Good thing we all have 2nd place credits!

hanna_banana: cha-ching

MACE1: buy em!

Everyone got the tyre upgrade. They refilled their supplies. Even after that, they still had plenty of credits left. So Mason and Hanna bought much-needed repairs.

hanna_banana: good 2 go!!! lets finish this!

ZKatt: can we do it tomrrw? i got a bunch of homework to finish

hanna_banana: thot u did hw before you play? isnt that yur dads rule??

ZKatt: usually but little bro wanted to go 2 park and dad was working. so not yet

K-EYE: I finished mine!

hanna_banana: lol obvi!! u r always mr. prepared

MACE1: lets race tmrrw thn

ZKatt: thx! l8r!

hanna_banana: ttfn!

Hanna signed off. She was disappointed to put off the final race. She was having such a good time with her squad. But OW had also kept her mind off something. The fact that the audition results would be posted the next day.

Would she get the lead? Or any part at all? It was going to be tough to sleep that night.

CHAPTER 9

THE BIG NEWS

"Let's get this over with," Hanna said to herself.

She marched to Mrs Bruening's classroom as soon as she got to school. The teacher had said she would post the cast list in the morning.

Drama students were crowding around the door. Hanna moved in. She read over their shoulders.

And . . .

Hanna didn't get the lead. It went to Erica.

Hanna braced herself for a wave of disappointment. It didn't come. Instead, she felt . . . relieved.

Hanna knew Erica was the best fit for the part. Hanna's time with her squad had taught her one big thing. What really mattered was doing what was best for the team. And Erica in the lead was best for the play. No question.

Hanna kept scanning the list. Then she spotted her name. She had got a part after all!

It was a small one, but still. She would be doing what she loved. And she hoped being in the play would help her to make more friends. To fit in with her new team.

Hanna smiled and went off to class. Along the way, she dug out her phone. She opened a chat with Zoe.

hanna_banana: hey

ZKatt: well???

hanna_banana: didnt get the lead

ZKatt: oh no! sorry :(

hanna_banana: its ok. got another part, Gertie

ZKatt: ?

hanna_banana: the lady wth the funny laugh

ZKatt: that sounds like a horse?!!

hanna_banana: lol yep! itll be fun!!!

ZKatt: rly? ur good?

hanna_banana: o yeah!!! that part always gets laughs n the show

ZKatt: and u shud do a good horse, growing up on a ranch lol

hanna_banana: u know it!!

Hanna put her phone away. She had almost got to her first class. Then she saw Erica coming round the corner up ahead.

"Hey!" Hanna called. "Congratulations on the lead!"

Erica rushed over. "Thanks! I'm really excited. And nervous!"

Erica shifted her backpack. "I was actually looking for you," she added. "I wanted to ask. Do you . . . think you could help me? With the part? I'm not sure about the accent. And there are a lot more lines than I'm used to. Since you've played Laurey before, you would be a huge help."

Hanna nodded and smiled. "Of course! And don't worry. You're going to be great!"

CHAPTER 10

LAST RACE

That night, Hanna joined her squad for the final race to the top! The guys had congratulated her on landing a part. Then everyone focused on the game. Zoe was live streaming again. Not only that, this race had the biggest credit payout of all! The squad was gunning for first.

Snow sprayed out from under Hanna's spiked tyres. The forest around the racers thinned out. The snow thickened. The cars struggled up the steep mountain.

Kai's van began to fall behind. Its armour was great for defence. But in the snow? The heavy vehicle was in trouble. Even with the tyre upgrade.

K-EYE: I think I picked the wrong car for this.

hanna_banana: i got u!

Hanna zipped ahead of Kai. She aimed her spear gun and fired. **FWOOP!** A cable spear hit the front of Kai's van.

K-EYE: You shot me! Again!

hanna_banana: yep. :) now hit the pedal!!!

The van's engine revved. The monster truck whined. Hanna towed Kai higher and higher. Soon, the track levelled out.

FWONK! Hanna dropped the cable. She and Kai caught up to the others.

MACE1: gg!

K-EYE: Thanks for the lift H!

hanna_banana: np we r a team remembr??

The squad raced into a dark tunnel. The icy track sparkled from their headlights. Then the tunnel opened to a tall cave. The track spiralled up around the walls.

They would be racing to the top of the mountain. From inside it! They started up the spiral track.

MACE1: harder to steer, is it jst me?

ZKatt: me 2!!!

Hanna felt the same. Her truck slid a bit with every turn. The icy path was slippery.

K-EYE: SO glad we got the tyres.

MACE1: just watch tht dropoff!

As if proving Mason's point, an NPC lost control on the ice. The car slid over the edge. It disappeared into darkness.

Hanna focused on the track. She didn't even think about attacking. Or passing. If she tried? She would go off the edge.

Luckily, the track soon led to another tunnel. Hanna let out the breath she was holding.

The squad raced into a wide cave. Tall ice columns rose up around them. It was like the forest all over again, but with ice.

MACE1: now we cn pass!

hanna_banana: and attack!!!

FWOP! Hanna fired a spear at an NPC. It missed the enemy. It hit a column instead.

CRASH! The ice fell and crushed the car flat!

ZKatt: nice!

MACE1: check ths out!

Mason pulled up between two enemy racers.

FWOOSH! Flames blasted from both sides of his car. The NPCs spun out of control.

hanna_banana: wOOt! now whos showin off??

MACE1: cant let u be the star all the time

hanna_banana: lol i guess ;)

The squad took out enemies left and right. There were no ramps for Zoe to jump. But she dropped bombs behind her. **BAM-BAM! BAM!** Trailing cars went up in flames.

Kai handed out supplies to the team as usual. But he got a few enemies too. He shoved one into an ice column. **CRASH!**

MACE1: gg! we got the lead!

K-EYE: Bunch of cars behind us though.

hanna_banana: bet yur followers <3 this Z!!!

ZKatt: def! my stream chat is blowin up!

MACE1: K mor flame fuel plz

K-EYE: On it.

Kai drove up to the front of the pack. He launched a giant fuel can at Mason's car.

MACE1: thx

K-EYE: Hey look, light ahead!

Sure enough, there was a bright light. It was the end of the tunnel. Beyond that, Hanna could just make out blue sky. And the final finish line.

MACE1: almost there!

K-EYE: We can win this!

As the squad zoomed closer, a jagged pit came into view. It split the ground between them and the tunnel's end. A small ramp was on their side.

MACE1: have to go 1 at a time. go for it K

K-EYE: Got it.

Kai's van raced forwards. It sped off the small ramp. **CRICK-CRUSHHH!** Then the ramp cracked and broke apart! The van sailed over the pit. Kai still made it to the finish line. But now there was no way for the others to cross.

K-EYE: Sorry!!!

ZKatt: what do we do??

hanna_banana: other cars r comin in fast!

MACE1: thnking...

Hanna was thinking too. There was an ice column by the pit. She had an idea. She almost acted on it. She even loaded a spear. But then she thought of Zoe and her live stream.

Instead of firing, Hanna typed a chat.

hanna_banana: Z! bomb that column!! it will fall and make a bridge

ZKatt: u spear it. my bombs only come out back

hanna_banana: no u go! drive up, brake, spin, drop bombs, BOOM!

ZKatt: rly?

hanna_banana: pro gamer move! u got it!

Zoe sped towards the column. Hanna got busy buying time for her teammate.

FWOP! FWOP-FWOP! FWOP! FWOP!

Hanna fired spears at the incoming enemy racers. She hit some cars. Others swerved and slowed.

At the same time, Zoe slammed her brakes and turned hard. Her buggy spun round. Its back was facing the column.

A bomb flew out of the buggy. It shot towards the tower of ice.

BOOM!

The column fell across the pit.

---

hanna_banana: U TTLY NAILED IT Z!!!

MACE1: GO GO GO

The rest of squad raced over the icy bridge. They burst out of the cave and straight to the finish line.

MACE1: GG!! another OW level complete!

K-EYE: Triple payout too for first place!

ZKatt: great idea H! why didnt u just spear it tho?

hanna_banana: your stream, ur the star!!! ;)

Hanna smiled. She was thrilled for her friend. Hanna didn't need to be the star. But she would help her team in any way she could. No matter if it was racing enemies in OW or helping her new drama department put on the best show ever!

BONUS ROUND

1. Think of a time when you were new to a school, team or other kind of group. How did it feel? What did you do to fit in? How long did it take for you to be comfortable around the other people?

2. Why did Hanna keep chasing the enemy flamethrower car in chapter 4? How did this decision affect the rest of the squad?

3. Hanna and Zoe each say they're sorry for how they have behaved. Think of a time when you apologized. Was it hard or easy? How did you feel afterwards?

4. In chapter 9, Hanna thinks that doing what's best for the team is what matters most. Do you agree? Why or why not?

5. Imagine if Hanna did get the starring role in the play. How would she react? Do you think she would take the role?

6. Hanna wants to be a good friend to her squad and to her classmate Erica. In what ways does she do that? Use examples from the story.

TAKING CARE

In real life, there may not be levels to beat. Or bosses to battle. But it can still be tough. Equip yourself with the tools and knowledge to take care of your mental health. Check out the online resources below. And don't ever be afraid to ask for help from friends, family or trusted adults.

BBC Bitesize:
www.bbc.co.uk/bitesize/articles/zmvt6g8

BBC Children in Need:
www.bbcchildreninneed.co.uk

Childline:
www.childline.org.uk

Health For Teens:
www.healthforteens.co.uk

Mental Health Foundation:
www.mentalhealth.org.uk

NHS Mental Health:
www.nhs.uk/mental-health/children-and-young-adults/mental-health-support/

Young Minds:
www.youngminds.org.uk/young-person/

GLOSSARY

announce tell something to many people; an announcement is information that is told to the public

audition tryout performance by an actor or performer in order to get a part

avatar character in a video game, chat room, app or other computer program that stands for and is controlled by a person

buggy small vehicle with large tyres made for off-road driving

depot building where many vehicles are kept

distraction something that draws your focus and keeps you from thinking about something else

dodge get out of the way by moving quickly

mission planned job or task

NPC character in a video game that cannot be controlled by a player; short for Non-Player Character or Non-Playable Character

repair fix and make something work again

swerve turn suddenly

upgrade something that makes a machine work better or adds a new and useful ability

THE AUTHOR

MICHAEL ANTHONY STEELE has been in the entertainment industry for more than 27 years, writing for television, films and video games. He has written more than 120 books for exciting characters and brands, including Batman, Superman, Wonder Woman, Spider-Man, Shrek and Scooby-Doo. Steele lives on a ranch in Texas, USA, but he enjoys meeting readers when he goes to visit schools and libraries across the United States. For more information, visit MichaelAnthonySteele.com.

THE ILLUSTRATOR

MIKE LAUGHEAD is a comics creator and illustrator of children's books, T-shirts, book covers and other fun things in the children's market. He has been doing that for almost 20 years. Mike is also an illustration instructor at Brigham Young University-Idaho, USA. He lives in Idaho with his amazing wife and three wonderful daughters. To see his portfolio, visit shannonassociates.com/mikelaughead